后羿射日

Houyi Shoots the Renegade Suns

　　传说在遥远而辽阔的东海边，生长着一棵神奇的扶桑树。那时候太阳不像现在一样只有一个，而是有十个。十个太阳像小鸟一样栖息在这棵大树上。这些太阳都是天帝的儿子，担负着照耀大地的责任。

　　天帝是个慈爱的父亲，很疼爱这十个顽皮的太阳孩子，但他严厉地告诫孩子：十个太阳必须轮流值班，每天一换，从东方升上天空，为人类带去光和热。所以，值班的太阳栖息在树梢上，剩下的九个太阳就栖息在较矮点的树枝上。

According to legend, there was a magic Fusang tree located at the ex-
treme limits of the broad eastern sea. At that time, there were ten suns rather
than one as it is today. Residing in the magic tree just like ten birds, the ten
suns together bore the responsibility for shining over the whole earth. They
were the children of the God of Heaven.

Being a loving father, the God of Heaven was very fond of the ten
naughty suns. However, he sternly warned them that each of them had to
take his turn to fulfill their duty and each day one of the sun was to travel
through the sky and light the world. So the sun on duty perched at
the top of the Fusang tree while the other suns were resting in
the branches below.

　　每当黎明来临时，当值的太阳就坐上两匹红色骏马拉着的白色的两轮车，威风凛凛地越过天空，洒出金色的光芒照耀人间的每个角落。

　　有了太阳，大地万物得以茁壮成长，人们因此有了食物，得到了温暖，生活和谐幸福。人们感恩太阳为他们带来了光明和欢乐。所以，太阳们都特别盼望着能够当值。

　　As dawn broke, the sun on duty would travel in state across the sky on a white chariot drawn by two red horses, illuminating every corner of the human world.

　　In the light from the sun, all things on the earth thrived, providing people with food. Warmed by the heat from the sunshine, everyone lived a happy life, and they were deeply grateful to the sun for bringing them light and joy. Therefore, the ten suns all looked forward to being on duty.

日复一日,年复一年。时间长了,太阳们慢慢地觉得这样的日子实在是太无聊了,他们想一起升上天空去玩。于是他们将天帝的告诫抛到脑后。这天早上,十个太阳一起爬上了两轮车,赶着骏马,笑着闹着就上了天空。

As the years passed, however, the suns grew tired of the old routine. Instead, they decided that all of them would rise at once. Having totally forgotten the God of Heaven's warning, one day the ten suns all ascended together on the chariot and began cavorting in the sky.

天空中一下子出现了十个太阳，生活在大地上的人和动物却受不了了。十个太阳就像十个大火球，发出炙热的阳光，大地就像着了火。好多天过去了，十个太阳每天都一起出来。这下可糟了，大地烤焦了，田里的庄稼枯死了，人们没有粮食可吃；河流干枯了，大海也几乎干涸，水里的鱼儿全死光了；森林着了火，许多动物被烧死了，没烧死的，也四下流窜，发疯似地找水找食物；人们忍受着高温，在火海中苦苦挣扎，没有吃的，还要防备野兽攻击，纷纷跪地祈求上苍让他们脱离苦海。

When the ten suns suddenly appeared together in the sky, the heat on earth made life unbearable for humans and animals alike. The suns were like ten blazing infernos, and the land seemed to burn. For many days the ten suns rose together in the east, and the heat on earth became ever more intense. As a result, the land was scorched and crops shriveled in the fields; people had nothing to eat; lakes and ponds dried up; no fish were left alive; forests were ablaze so that many animals were burned to death, and those which barely survived ran away crazed, looking for water and food. The people, tortured and driven to desperation by the heat, fire, hunger and rampaging beasts, prayed on bended knees for divine intervention.

天帝看到了人间的情况,非常生气,决定教训一下他的儿子。于是,他叫来了后羿,让他下凡驱逐他们。
　　后羿是个年轻的神仙,生来就有射箭的天赋,长大后更是臂力过人。他接受了天帝交给他的使命,来到了人间。

Angered by the suffering of the human world, the God of Heaven decided to teach his sons a lesson for their misdeeds. So he sent for Houyi, a god of archery, to descend to the earth to drive them out.

Houyi was a young god, born to be a super-skilled archer, who had developed very strong arms. He accepted the mission and descended from the heavens to aid Mankind.

后羿被眼前的景象惊呆了，他不敢相信，这个焦□的、满目疮痍的世界就是以前那个充满生机与欢□的人间。被太阳们折磨得奄奄一息的人们见到后□，纷纷跪地请求后羿解救他们。

愤怒的后羿举头望向天空，只见十个火辣辣的□阳正肆无忌惮地挂在高空，比赛谁能释放出最强□热浪，丝毫不顾地上人们的死活。后羿下定决心，无论多么困难，他□要把人们从苦难中解救出来。

Houyi was shocked by what he saw. He could not bear to believe that □e scorched and devastated land was the human world which had been □lled with vitality and joy. The people, severely tortured by the scorching □eat of the ten suns, got on their knees to beg Houyi to save them.

Houyi was enraged by what he found. He looked up at the sky and □aw the ten scorching suns hanging shamelessly in the upper air, competing □ith one another to produce the most incandescent waves of heat in total □isregard of the welfare of the mortals on earth. Houyi had made up his □ind, no matter how difficult, to save Mankind from further suffering.

后羿背上一张红色的神弓、十支白色神箭就出发了。他要爬上东海边最高的山上最高的山峰，用他的神弓神箭将那几个骄横的太阳射下来。

后羿爬过了九十九座高山，渡过了九十九条河流，穿越了九十九个峡谷，忍着饥饿，不顾劳累，终于来到了东海边。他爬上了海边最高的山顶，这是离太阳们最近的地方。

Houyi set out with a divine red bow and ten divine white arrows. He wanted to mount the summit of the highest mountain at the limits of the eastern sea and, from there, shoot down those arrogant suns with his divine bow and arrows.

Houyi climbed over ninety-nine mountains, crossed ninety-nine rivers, and went through ninety-nine valleys, enduring the torments of hunger and hardship, until he finally arrived at the limits of the eastern sea. He ascended the summit by the sea and stood on the place in all the earth which was closest to the suns.

后羿迎着刺眼的光芒高声对太阳们喊道:"不要再危害人间了,立刻回到你们该待的地方去。"

太阳们才不把后羿放在眼里,照样一齐在天空逞威逞强,他们蛮横地说:"不费吹灰之力,我们连整个人间万物都能烤焦,还怕你么?"

后羿大怒,拉开万斤重的大弓,搭上万斤重的利箭,瞄准了天上火辣辣的太阳。

太阳们一齐放射出万丈光芒,如同万千支金色的利剑,刺得后羿睁不开眼睛;他们一齐释放出巨大的热能,如同万千个火炉,烤得后羿的身体非常疼。

Facing the dazzling light, Houyi shouted to the suns, "Don't harm the human world any more; go back where you came from now."

The suns ignored Houyi's advice. As usual they rose into the sky at once, showing off their power. They rudely said, "We can very easily scorch the whole world; how can we fear you?"

Houyi erupted with anger. He nocked a divine arrow in the divine bow and aimed at the suns in the sky. The suns all together sent out brilliant rays which, like thousands of golden swords, stabbed at Houyi's eyes; together they radiated enormous heat which, like thousands of furnaces, burnt Houyi all over.

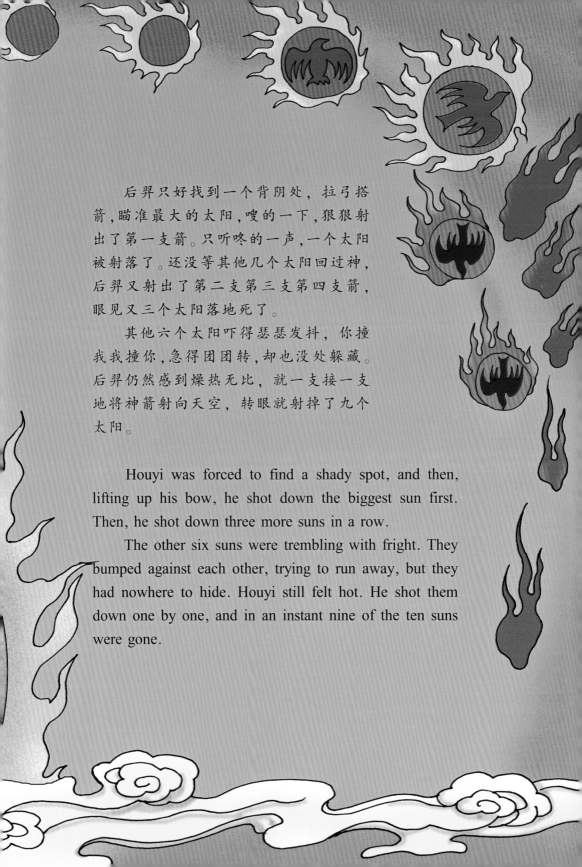

后羿只好找到一个背阴处，拉弓搭箭，瞄准最大的太阳，嗖的一下，狠狠射出了第一支箭。只听咚的一声，一个太阳被射落了。还没等其他几个太阳回过神，后羿又射出了第二支第三支第四支箭，眼见又三个太阳落地死了。

其他六个太阳吓得瑟瑟发抖，你撞我我撞你，急得团团转，却也没处躲藏。后羿仍然感到燥热无比，就一支接一支地将神箭射向天空，转眼就射掉了九个太阳。

Houyi was forced to find a shady spot, and then, lifting up his bow, he shot down the biggest sun first. Then, he shot down three more suns in a row.

The other six suns were trembling with fright. They bumped against each other, trying to run away, but they had nowhere to hide. Houyi still felt hot. He shot them down one by one, and in an instant nine of the ten suns were gone.

最后剩下的小太阳害怕极了，不断向后羿讨饶，保证以后再也不做危害人间的事了。此时后羿觉得凉快多了，他想，人间也确实需要一个太阳给大地带来光和热，于是就放过了最后一个太阳。但他告诫这个太阳一定要兢兢业业为人类服务。从此，这个太阳每天早上从东海边升起，傍晚从西山落下，为人间带来光明，让万物和谐生存。

The last surviving sun was terrified; he kept begging Houyi for mercy, promising not to cause mischief again. By this time, Houyi felt much cooler. He thought that if he killed the last sun the world would be left in total darkness, so he let him go. But he cautioned him to be sure to serve Mankind well. From then on, every day the sun has risen at dawn in the east and set at dusk in the west, bringing light to the human world, making all things on earth exist in a harmonious way.

　　天帝知道后羿射杀了他的九个太阳儿子后，非常恼怒。他的本意只是想教训一下太阳孩子，没想到后羿却违抗天命。于是天帝惩罚后羿，将他贬到人间，永远不准再回天庭。

　　后羿射掉了九个太阳后，人们恢复了日出而作、日落而息的生活。大家纷纷称颂后羿是为民除害的英雄。

The God of Heaven was annoyed with Houyi for shooting down the nine suns, nine of his errant children, instead of merely giving them some sort of punishment as he had wished. The God of Heaven could not forgive Houyi. So Houyi was banished from the heavens and forbidden ever to return.

Still, since Houyi had killed nine suns and restored people to their normal lives, everyone on earth praised Houyi as a savior who had done a heroic deed for Mankind.

End